HEllooooO

FOR PETER AND MATHEW

Henry Holt and Company, LLC
Publishers since 1866
175 Fifth Avenue
New York, New York 10010
mackids.com

First published in the United States in 2013 by Henry Holt and Company, LLC.
Originally published in the United Kingdom in 2012 by Gullane Children's Books.

Library of Congress Cataloging-in-Publication Data
Massini, Sarah.
Trixie ten / Sarah Massini. — 1st American ed.
p.   cm.
Summary: The youngest of ten children, Trixie grows tired of all the noise and sets off on her own to find a quiet place.
ISBN 978-0-8050-9520-3 (hardcover)
[1. Brothers and sisters—Fiction. 2. Family life—Fiction. 3. Noise—Fiction. 4. Runaways—Fiction.] I. Title.
PZ7.M423857Tri 2013   [E]—dc23   2012011487

First American Edition—2013
Printed in China by Imago Shenzhen, Luohu District, Shenzhen

10 9 8 7 6 5 4 3 2 1

TRIXIE
TEN

SARAH MASSINI

Henry Holt and Company
New York

This is
Trixie TEN.
She has nine brothers and sisters.
She thinks they are all very annoying.

Wanda ONE
is always sneezing.

Thomas TWO
has the hiccups.

Theo THREE
burps—and loudly!

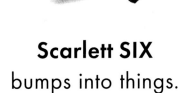

Florence FOUR
giggles and giggles.

Felix FIVE
laughs all the time.

Scarlett SIX
bumps into things.

Sammy SEVEN
is always surprised.

Emily EIGHT
has a runny nose
but never, ever
a Kleenex.

Nathaniel NINE
is the most annoying of all.
He likes pretending
to be a lion.

At nighttime, to make sure they are all safe and sound and tucked up in their ten little beds, Trixie and her brothers and sisters count themselves in:

**Wanda
ONE**

**Thomas
TWO**

**Theo
THREE**

**Florence
FOUR**

**Felix
FIVE**

**Scarlett
SIX**

**Sammy
SEVEN**

**Emily
EIGHT**

**Nathaniel
NINE**

**Trixie
TEN**

Trixie tries to sleep. But . . .

"**Nine** brothers and sisters are **so noisy!**" Trixie sighs.

It isn't any quieter during the day.
"**Nine** brothers and sisters are **too noisy!**" sighs Trixie.
"And they take up **too much room!**"

One day, Trixie decides to leave.
She packs some useful things
into a useful bag:

ONE useful flashlight,

ONE useful teddy bear,

ONE useful blanket.

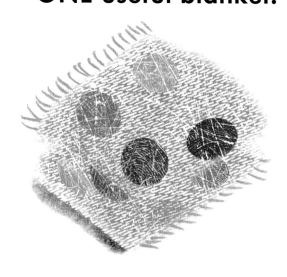

HIC
HIC
HAHA
HIC
TCHOOOOOO OO
ROAR
OW

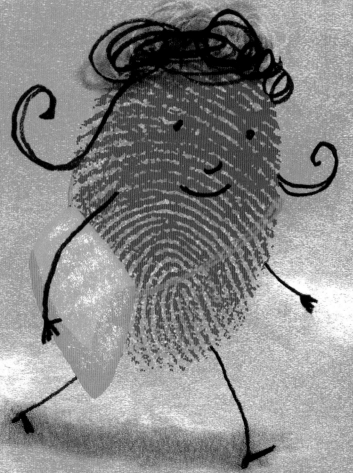

And when no one is looking,
she creeps away in search of
somewhere quiet.

She walks and walks until . . .

. . . she comes to a stream.

But the stream isn't quiet—it is full of babbling fish!
"These are my **nine** brothers and sisters," says a fish.
"You're **very noisy** . . . for fish!"
"That's just the way we are!" the fish says proudly.

Trixie says good-bye to the fish.
She walks and walks until . . .

BUBBLE

BUBBLE

BUBBLE

BUBBLE

BUBBLE

BUBBLE

. . . she comes to a meadow.

"So many rabbits!" says Trixie.
They take up **so much room!**
"These are my **ninety-nine** brothers and sisters,"
says the rabbit happily.

Trixie counts them. It takes a *long* time.
"Maybe **nine** brothers and sisters aren't so
many after all," she thinks.

Trixie says good-bye to the rabbits.
She walks and walks until . . .

. . . she finds a
big, empty, quiet place.

Nighttime comes,
Silent and still.
Trixie takes out her useful flashlight. She hugs her useful teddy bear,
and she counts the spots on her useful blanket.

She begins to think about
Wanda and Thomas and Theo and Florence and Felix,
Scarlett, Sammy, Emily, and Nathaniel.
She wishes she had someone to talk to.
She wishes she wasn't **so alone**.

Meanwhile, Trixie's brothers and sisters
are counting themselves into bed.
Is everyone all tucked in?
Is everyone safe and sound?

Wanda
ONE

Thomas
TWO

Theo
THREE

Florence
FOUR

Felix
FIVE

Scarlett
SIX

Sammy
SEVEN

Emily
EIGHT

Nathaniel
NINE

...?

"Where is Trixie TEN?"

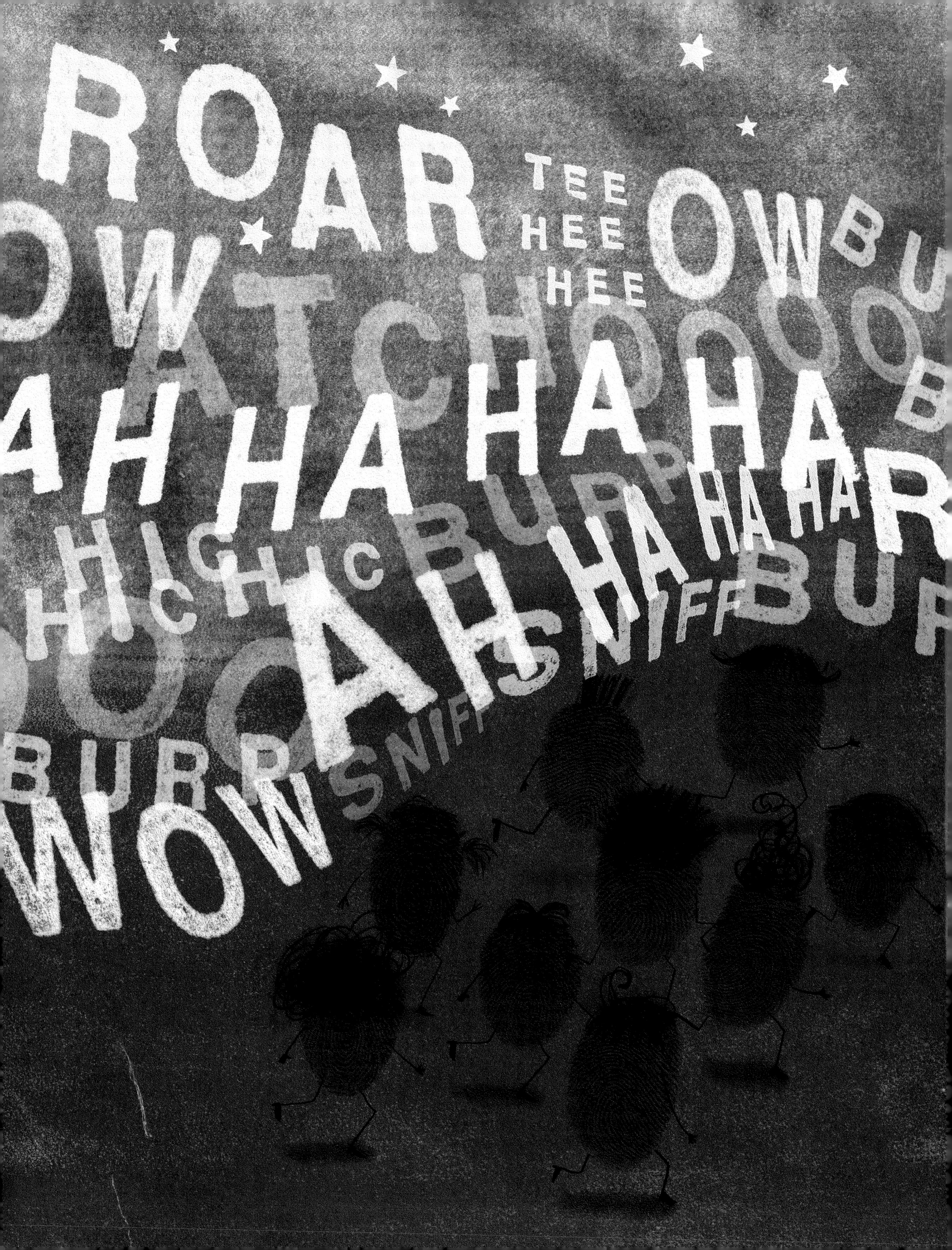

ROAR
TEE HEE HEE
OW
OW
ATCHOOOO
AH HA HA HA
HIC HIC
HIC HIC
BURP
HA HA HA HA
AH
SNIFF
SNIFF
SNIFF
BURP
BURP
WOW

ROAR AH HA HA HA HA BURP WOW OW HIC
BURP WOW SNIFF ATCHOOO HIC
TEE HEE HEE OW SNIFF WOW BURP
SNIFF OW HIC HEE HIC

It is very dark outside
and very, very scary.
But they bravely go in search of Trixie Ten.
They walk and walk until . . .

"It's me!" cries Trixie,
switching on her useful flashlight.
"I heard you coming!"

"Please come home," her **nine**
brothers and sisters say.
"We miss you!"
"I miss you too,"
says Trixie. **"A lot!"**
So they all make
their **noisy** way
back home . . .

. . . and count themselves into bed:

**Wanda
ONE**

**Thomas
TWO**

**Theo
THREE**

**Florence
FOUR**

**Scarlett
SIX**

**Sammy
SEVEN**

**Emily
EIGHT**

**Nathaniel
NINE**

CHOOOO

BURP BUR

OW

HIC AH HA HA HA

HIC

BURP

WOW

ROAR

TEE HEE HEE

AH HA HA

SNI

Felix
FIVE

Trixie
TEN

It is just as **noisy** as usual.
"But that's the way we are,"
thinks Trixie.

And she drifts happily
off to sleep.